Godiva

by Lynn Cullen

illustrated by Kathryn Hewitt

 A Golden Book • New York
Golden Books Publishing Company, Inc.
New York, New York 10106

Thanks to Neela, Jamie, Hannah, and Molly,
and my dramatic family, and friends. K.H.

Library of Congress Cataloging-in-Publication Data
Cullen, Lynn.
Godiva / by Lynn Cullen ; illustrated by Kathryn Hewitt.
p. cm.
Summary: With only her long hair as a cloak,
Lady Godiva takes her heroic ride through the English village of Coventry
in exchange for her husband's promise to lower the people's taxes.
ISBN 0-307-41175-3 (alk. paper)
1. Godiva, Lady, circa 1040–1080—Legends. [1. Godiva, Lady, circa 1040–1080—Legends.
2. Folklore—England.] I. Hewitt, Kathryn, ill. II. Title.
PZ8.1.C894 Go 2001   398.2'0942'02—dc21   [E]   00–046252

The illustrations for this book were created with oils on paper.

For Lauren
—L. C.

For Morgan and Miles
—K. H.

Long ago, when fairies were as common in England as butterflies, there lived a young lord named Leofric. Lord Leofric had everything: A towering palace. More cattle than he could count. So much land it took days to cross—even on the fastest horse, which he owned.

One Christmas Day, Lord Leofric sat on his throne and raised his golden goblet to the common folk gathered in his Great Hall. "To Happiness!" he exclaimed.

The common folk raised their wooden cups and shouted back, "To Happiness!" Laughing and singing, they fell to their feast—the scraps from Lord Leofric's table.

Lord Leofric frowned. "These people seem much too merry," he told his most trusted servant. "I am far, far richer than all of them put together, yet they chortle and sing and carry on so. What have they got that I do not?"

His servant thought for a moment, then bowed. "Sire, perhaps it is time you find a bride."

"Do you suggest," Lord Leofric demanded, "that an important man like me could possibly be lonely?"

The servant said nothing, while below, the people broke into a dance.

Lord Leofric gazed at the laughing dancers. "Oh, very well," he said. "But if I must take a wife, she shall be the finest one in all England."

The next day, Lord Leofric took up his horse, whistled for his dog, and began his travels from manor to manor, seeking the perfect bride. But finding a bride was not as simple as Lord Leofric thought. None of the women brought forth was quite right. They would either laugh too much or too little. Hiccup after meals. Beat him at chess. At last, after many months, he gave up in despair and headed for home.

In a village not far from his palace, Lord Leofric stopped at a well. He handed his flask to a girl filling her own bucket. "Draw me some water," he said, "and do hurry. My journey has been long and I am thirsty."

The girl took his flask without a word and began filling it. Just then, a wind swept across the fields, flapping the sleeves of her gown. Lord Leofric's dog, startled by the sudden movement, jumped up and nipped at the maiden. Lord Leofric scolded the dog, then turned to the girl. "You must excuse Arthur. Sometimes dogs can be very bad."

"Oh no, sir," said the girl. "Dogs are quite good. They give us pups. Do you know of anything more dear than a pup?"

Lord Leofric drew back. Never had anyone the nerve to disagree with him. But before he could respond, a bee sailed around his head. He batted it away. "Terrible creature!"

"Oh no, sir," said the girl. "Bees give us honey. Do you know of anything so sweet?"

Lord Leofric stared at the girl. Did she not know who he was? But before he could tell her, a dark cloud let loose its rain.

"Curse this rain!" cried Leofric, plucking at his robe. "It will ruin my velvet."

The girl lifted her face to the rain. "Bless the rain. It gives us flowers."

Lord Leofric peered at the girl. "Who *are* you?"

"I am Godiva," she said, "the cobbler's daughter."

"Godiva," Lord Leofric whispered. He looked both this way and that for fairies. Surely one had put a spell on him! For at this moment he knew he must have this daughter of a cobbler for his wife.

And so the wedding was arranged. Godiva was crowned with a golden circlet, seated upon a throne, and a feast was proclaimed. All the common folk gathered in the Great Hall. "To Happiness!" said Lord Leofric, raising his golden goblet.

"To Happiness!" the folk called back.

And Lord Leofric, gazing at his lovely new wife, thought that at last happiness was his.

Wishing to please Godiva, Lord Leofric set to work on improving his palace. He spent his days inspecting new tapestries for the walls, ordering golden benches for the Great Hall, and purchasing carved chests for the bedchamber.

Meanwhile, Godiva rode to the nearest village, Coventry, where she admired the pups of the tailor's faithful hound. Found honeycombs with the goose girl. Made garlands of roses for the weaver's widow's children.

"You glow with happiness," said Lord Leofric over supper one night. Thinking he must be the cause of her joy, he asked shyly, "What brings your smile?"

"I was recalling my day with the villagers," said Godiva.

"You mustn't waste time with them," snapped Lord Leofric. "Don't you see they are only kind to you because of our gold?"

Godiva frowned at her apple tart. "I do not think—"

"Enough!" cried Lord Leofric. "The sooner you understand that we are we and they are they, the sooner you will understand the way of the world. Look out for yourself," he said, patting the furred front of his robe. "That is the way to true happiness."

Weeks rolled into months. Towers grew from the palace walls as the wheat ripened upon the land. Though Lord Leofric forbade it, Godiva still rode into Coventry to visit the people. But as harvest time neared, she noticed that the weaver's widow's children were growing thinner. The tailor's son was dressed in rags. Indeed, all the children of the village were in tatters.

"Why are the children so thin?" Godiva asked the weaver's widow. "And where are their warm clothes?"

The weaver's widow gazed upon her own chapped hands. "Dear Lady," she said at last, "your Lord has demanded more money from us to better his palace. We have little left for ourselves."

Godiva galloped back to the palace and marched straight to Lord Leofric. "My lord," she demanded, "why are you taking more money from the people?"

Lord Leofric shrugged. "How else am I to give you a fine palace?"

"I do not need a fine palace!" Godiva exclaimed. "You must lower their taxes."

Lord Leofric laughed. "Dear Godiva, the day I lower taxes is the day you ride naked through the streets of Coventry."

Godiva stared at him. "You would do that?" she asked.

"Lower taxes if you ride naked?" Lord Leofric chuckled. "Of course! Both are equally unthinkable."

Godiva drew herself up. "I shall ride tomorrow at noon."

Lord Leofric turned pale. "You can't. The people will laugh and point their fingers. Oh, the pleasure they will get from bringing us low!"

"I shall ride," said Godiva.

"Why do you do this for them? Never once have they lifted a finger for us unless I bid them so."

"I shall ride," Godiva said once more.

Outside the window, the goose girl, who had followed her goose to the palace, heard all. She ran to the village and told the weaver's widow, then the weaver's widow told the baker's wife, and the baker's wife told the miller. "The Lady rides naked at noon," they whispered. "Lord Leofric will lower our taxes if she does." The word was repeated until it came at last to Tom, the tailor's son.

"Naked?" Tom piped. "The Lady would do that for us?"

The next day at noon, true to her word, Godiva removed her robes until her only cloak was that of her long burnished gold hair. She climbed upon her horse and, followed by a tight-jawed Leofric, rode into Coventry.

Clip clop! Clip clop! went the hooves of Godiva's horse. *Clip clop! Clip clop!* went the hooves of Lord Leofric's horse behind them.

Godiva gazed at her horse's mane. "I do this for my loved ones," she whispered to herself. "For them, I must endure."

"Hurry!" Lord Leofric hissed behind her. "You make a fool of yourself!"

Then, over the steady *clip clop, clip clop,* Godiva heard another sound. *Clack.* From both sides of the street, from as far ahead as she could hear. *Clack. Clack clack.*

Godiva looked up. All through the village, people were pulling their shutters closed. She broke into a smile. "They turn away."

Leofric didn't know whether to rejoice or shout in anger. He spied a boy standing in front of a window. "What ho!" he shouted. "A peeper! I shall put his eyes out."

"No!" Godiva told her husband. To the boy she called, "Good day, Tom!"

"Is that my Lady?" called out the boy. He broke into a smile. "We love you, Lady!"

Godiva threw back her head and laughed with joy.

Just then a small shriek came from within the cottage. Tom was pulled from sight and the shutter slammed shut.

"How can you laugh?" snapped Lord Leofric. "That boy saw you in your nakedness."

Godiva gave her husband a patient smile. "God bless Tom, the tailor's son. He has been blind since birth."

And so it was, three miracles happened that day. Godiva rode naked through her village unseen. Lord Leofric lowered taxes. And Lord Leofric found there is something people treasure more than gold: kindness.

In time, Godiva bore Lord Leofric a baby boy. With her husband's blessing, she often brought her son to the village to play with the goose girl, the weaver's widow's children, and Tom, the tailor's son. When all would gather at feasts, Lord Leofric, sharing his finest food, would raise his cup and shout, "To Happiness!"

And the people would call back, "To Happiness!"

And indeed, Lord Leofric was happy, his heart as light as the butterflies flitting through the air like fairies.

Author's Note

THE LEGEND of Godiva's ride through Coventry has been told for nearly a thousand years. Like all good legends, it is based in fact. Though Godiva's birthdate is unknown, records show she was married to Leofric, lord of the Anglo-Saxon earldom of Mercia, before he died in 1057. Historians have also documented that Godiva convinced her husband to found monasteries at Coventry and Stow, but the evidence behind her famous ride remains hazy.

The oldest written version of the tale was recorded by Roger of Wendover sometime before his death in 1236, though he claimed to be quoting earlier writers. By the fifteenth century, Peeping Tom had popped into the story. Traditionally, Tom the tailor was the only person in Coventry who dared to gaze upon the naked Godiva, and for his wickedness, he instantly went blind. I preferred to make Tom younger and already blind, to refocus on the original tale of Godiva's sacrifice for her people, and to emphasize that even sightless, Tom could see more clearly than Lord Leofric.

Though the true story of Godiva ended when she died in 1080, the people of Coventry have remained grateful to her through the centuries. They instituted a festival in her honor in 1678 as part of their annual fair, and to this day a statue of the Lady stands in a park in the center of the city.